Me, All Alone, at the End of the World

M. T. Anderson

illustrated by

Kevin Hawkes

CANDLEWICK PRESS

Text copyright © 2005 by M. T. Anderson
Illustrations copyright © 2005 by Kevin Hawkes

First edition in this format 2017

The Library of Congress has cataloged the original hardcover edition as follows:

Anderson, M. T.
Me, all alone, at the end of the world / M. T. Anderson ; illustrated by Kevin Hawkes. — 1st ed. 2005
p.   cm.
Summary: A boy enjoys living quietly by himself at the End of the World until
Mr. Constantine Shimmer, "Professional Visionary," builds an inn and an
amusement park, demanding that tourists come and have "Fun Without End!"
ISBN 978-0-7636-1586-4 (original hardcover)
[1. Solitude — Fiction. 2. Amusement parks — Fiction.] I. Hawkes, Kevin, ill. II. Title.
PZ7.A54395Ju 2005

[Fic] — dc21   2002034858

ISBN 978-0-7636-8902-5 (midi hardcover)

16 17 18 19 20 21 CCP 10 9 8 7 6 5 4 3 2 1

Printed in Shenzhen, Guangdong, China

This book was typeset in Quercus.
The illustrations were done in watercolor and acrylic.

Candlewick Press
99 Dover Street
Somerville, Massachusetts 02144

visit us at www.candlewick.com

To my cousin Mark,
who took me hang-gliding
at the End of the World
M. T. A.

To Hugh and Joyce,
extraordinary cliff dwellers
K. H.

I lived by myself at
the End of the World.

The days were slow and fine. I looked
for treasure with old maps from fallen empires.
I dusted off rocks and found fossils. I put the
bones of long monsters back together with
twine. I played ball by the drop. I sat and I
read. I liked to listen to wind from the empty
spaces blow through the bristly pines. The
branches swayed in the blue. I ate hardtack
and gristle. At sunset, I whistled dance tunes to
the mule.

On loud, stormy nights, I liked my shack.
I liked to lie cozy near the brass-bellied stove,
and hear the rain and the thunder fall, and the
chuckling beasts with long tails or five legs or
big kissing mouths squirm over the edge to
go snapping at lightning. I was never afraid.
I would fall asleep, hearing them growl in
voices like plumbing. I was happy there all by
myself, alone at the End of the World.

Until one day. That day as I sat, dangling my
legs off the world's edge, I saw a strange man.
He was a long-leggedy man with a wide, wide
hat and a beard in a circle around his head.
His glasses reflected the clouds.

He set up an easel. On it he painted the sky and the loneliest pine. And he said in a voice like wool from dream-sheep, "I am named Mr. Shimmer. Professional Visionary." He looked me up and looked me down. "Boy, what do you do all day by the world's end?"

"Oh, sir," I said, "lots of things." And I told him about whistling, gristle, and watching the bristly pines.

"That's all?" asked Shimmer. "Don't you have fun? Don't you have friends?"

I looked at my feet. It had always seemed fun. But now, I didn't know.

"I think," said Shimmer, "things are going to change around here."

Over his picture he painted the words CONSTANTINE SHIMMER'S GALVANO-MAGICAL END OF THE WORLD TOURS. FUN ALL THE TIME!

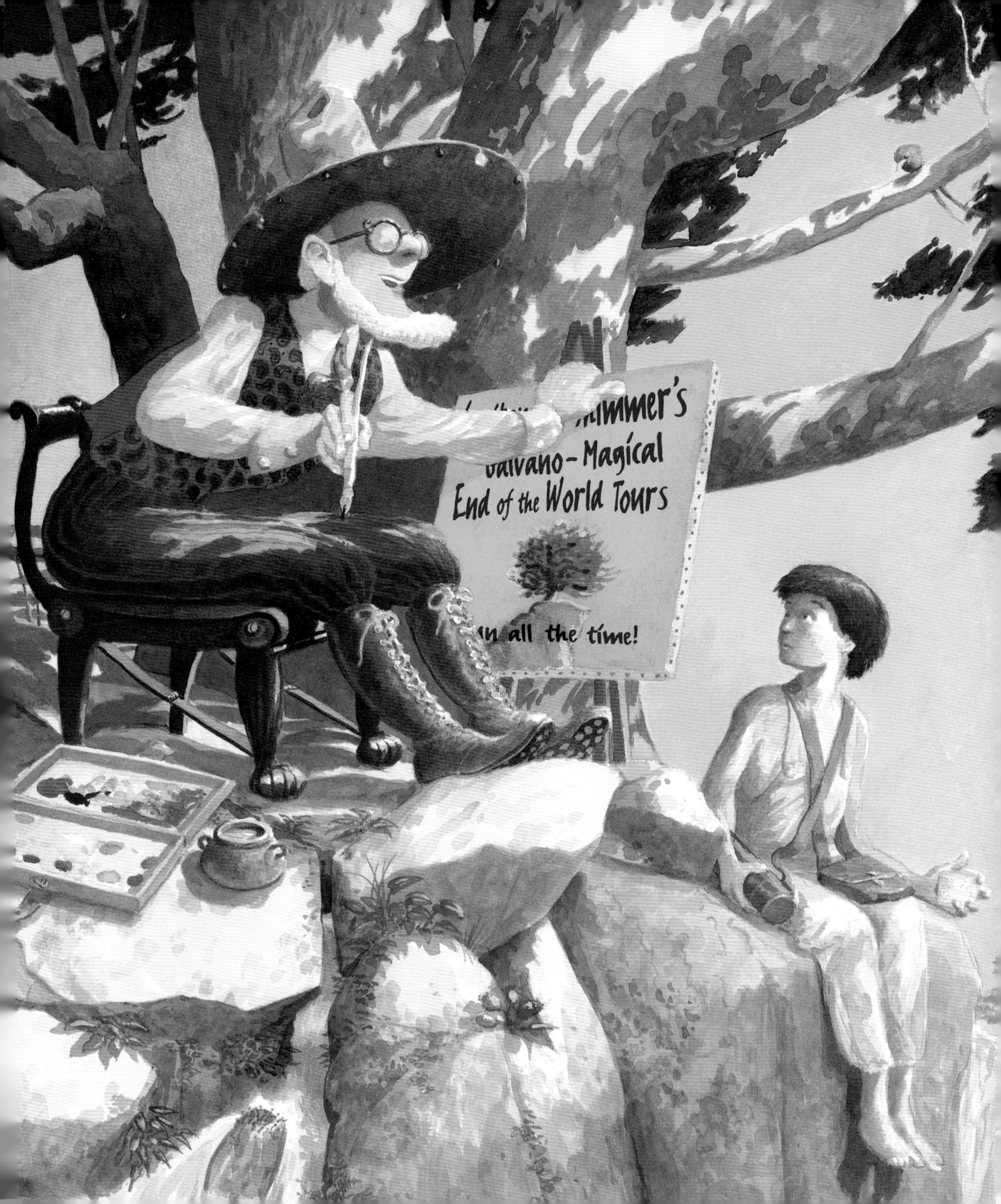
End of the World Tours
all the time!

A week later, I was netting fish that flew over the Rumblous Tumble-Up Falls when I heard big machines and men giving orders. They were paving a clearing. They were digging ditches. And tall Mr. Shimmer was leading a tour.

"Here," said Shimmer, "is the End of the World. Here is the cliff. Here is a lonely local boy with his mule. Notice their misty-eyed look. And here is the future site of the Inn at the End of the World."

I stood stock-still. A small crowd of parents and children was staring at me and the End of the World. They gawked at the cliff.

I could not believe Mr. Shimmer had flattened the ground. "Mr. Constantine Shimmer?" I piped. I pointed to the paving stones. "What are you doing? What have you done?"

"I've brought you some friends," said Constantine Shimmer. "If you show them the sights, I will give you a shiny doubloon."

"Sights?" I said. "I just live here alone in a shack. I don't need friends and I don't need . . ."

But then I looked at the kids who stood around Shimmer. They were smiling and nice. They held out their hands. One was named Bert, and one was named Juke, and one was named Minnie Bucket. They wanted to like me. I wanted to like them. I started to smile.

"Well," I said to the kids, "what can I show you?"

"What do you do around here?" they asked.

I thought of what I did: fossils, sunsets. "Um," I said. Whistling. The gristle. The bristly pines. "Er . . ." I tried to think of something that might be exciting. "Well, if you spit off the edge of the earth, the spit gob goes forever," I said.

"Wow," said Bert, and "Zowie!" said Juke, and Minnie Bucket cried, "This is electric!"

So we spent the day in the woods by the cliffs. We spat and we clapped. I pointed to fossils. I showed them the paths. I showed them the trees. I showed them the footprints from slithery beasties.

When the time came for them to go back to the city, they said, "We don't want to leave. We'll come see you this fall, when the Inn at the End of the World is complete."

As the fall came, Constantine Shimmer finished his inn. He put on the gables and porches and steeples. One by one, the leaves fell from trees and drifted off the edge. I liked to watch them spinning there. They fell through the sky under my feet.

And when
the colors were
really bright,
Bert and Juke
and Minnie Bucket came back
from the city, and we ran through the Inn at
the End of the World, and we played with the
elevators, and they sent out for room-service
turkey and chitlins and gum.

We rented four gliders from Shimmer's
Hang-Glidery, and swooped from the cliffs at
the end of the earth. We screamed as the blood
all rushed to our feet.

"Stash your tears!" cried Shimmer from land.
"Put aside mope! It is time now for fun! Ladies
and gentlemen, hop into line! Swoop for today
and forget your tomorrow!"

In the winter, snow fell on the trees and the cliffs and the tombs. I watched the flakes fall silent on the land. One day, a sleigh pulled up, and there were Minnie Bucket and Bert and Juke. We spat in our hands and shook and we winked.

We had a great time. We watched shadow puppets at night while wind blew. We rented ice skates from the Shimmer O-Frost-A-Thon and made figure eights by the Rumblous Tumble-Up Falls and figure nines on the Lake at the Drop. People were screaming and swinging on pines. Guests now were skating and skiing in numbers, flashing down slopes to great jumps and long ramps.

"What is fun? *This* is fun!" cried Shimmer from shore.

"Fun chock-a-block to your eyes and your teeth! Loneliness, ladies and lads? Gone, all gone at the Shimmer Inn Wintertime Ski and Skating Extravagorganza!"

Juke and Bert and Minnie Bucket came again in the spring. We couldn't hear the wind whistling through the bristly pines. The noise of the parties was too loud in the woods. Men with mustaches gave fox-trot lessons to duchesses and dry-cleaning heiresses wound up in silk.

The monsters did not come up for the lightning during spring rains anymore. They were afraid of the noise and the engines. Bert and Juke and Minnie Bucket and I ran on the paths through the woods, paths littered with noise-sticks and razzers and horns. We played hide-and-go-seek and tip-the-whole-hoosegow.

The shack where I lived was surrounded by buggies. I could no longer find the bones of long monsters; I could no longer find ancient gold. The pavilions and escalators covered them up.

In the summer, the crowds were enormous and the inn was open for honeymoon couples who came for the four-hour sunsets, but the sunsets weren't clear through the haze on the boardwalk with all the lights from the games, which we played.

We played Hurl the Gopher and Stumbling
Ted; we played Bite the Bullet and Axe to the
Grindstone and Blade-O-Matic Mumblypeg.
We spun in the Gravitron till Bert got the dry
heaves. We jumped from the ropes at the
Shimmer Yow-Gulf-O-Drop. We hung in the
ruins of the Sideways City, while sporty men in
striped Shimmer Scramble-Sweaters bounded
and vaulted from arches and domes.

"More fun!" bellowed Shimmer through
his bullhorn. "No solemn silences here at the
End of the World! Nothing but laughter!
And jumping! Madams, sirs — I highly
recommend vertigo!"

I hadn't slept for seven days. There now was a Ferris wheel over the gulf; there now was a towering tower; there now were some fireworks blasting the clouds, and statues that talked and that walked in the park.

Over the noise I yelled to my friends. "You know — I've been thinking. . . ."

"There's no time for thinking!" cried Shimmer from his podium, as the lights in his beard flashed and whirled. "It's time for some funning, not thinking! Observe, folks, the End of the World! The splendid, resplendent, sublime view from here! Isn't it lovely! I'll build a new deck where you can eat dinner! I'll make you some go-carts! Some blimp-sleds! Some capsules! Whatever you wish, I will build! Gentlemen, ladies — there is not a moment for gloom or for thought! *We shall have FUN! That's FUN without END!*"

Minnie was sweaty. "Come on!" she cried, tugging at my wrist.

"Here we come!" hollered Juke.

"Here we go!" giggled Bert, gnashing his teeth and rending his shirt.

"Um," I said. "Um, I think it's time for me to go." I lifted the sparkler-hat off my head. I turned off my shock-mittens. I rolled them up and gave them to Juke.

I said, "I've got to leave."

I said, "I miss the wind."

So I left.

Now I live all alone at the Top of
the World. It's a very tall
mountain. I can see to the
edge. The days are slow and
fine. I eat hardtack and gristle. I dust the rocks
and find fossils. I look for treasure with old
maps of fallen empires.

I sit on the porch of my shack and write
letters to my friends from the city, Bert and
Juke and Minnie Bucket. Someday soon I will
go and visit them.

In the afternoons, I listen to the wind from
the empty spaces blow through the bristly
pines.

I feel the soft loneliness of the world falling
in shadow.

For the time being,
I am happy here, here by myself
at the Top of the World, all alone.

M. T. ANDERSON is the author of many distinguished books for children and young adults, most recently *Symphony for the City of the Dead: Dmitri Shostakovich and the Siege of Leningrad.* He has also written two picture-book biographies: *Strange Mr. Satie: Composer of the Absurd,* illustrated by Petra Mathers, and *Handel, Who Knew What He Liked,* illustrated by Kevin Hawkes, which is a *Boston Globe–Horn Book* Honor winner. He is the author of the National Book Award–winning *The Astonishing Life of Octavian Nothing, Traitor to the Nation, Volume I: The Pox Party* and its follow-up, *Volume II: The Kingdom on the Waves.* His novel *Feed* was a National Book Award Finalist. M. T. Anderson lives in Cambridge, Massachusetts.

KEVIN HAWKES is the illustrator of more than forty acclaimed picture books and chapter books, including the *New York Times* best-selling *Library Lion* by Michelle Knudsen, *The Three Mouths of Little Tom Drum* by Nancy Willard, and *Weslandia* and *Sidewalk Circus,* both by Paul Fleischman. *Weslandia* was short-listed for the Kate Greenaway Medal. Kevin Hawkes lives in southern Maine with his family.